· C O N T E N T S ·

©2004 Robert Frederick Limited
4-5 North Parade
Bath, U.K.
BA1 1LF

Enid Blyton™
Magical Stories

illustrated by
Pam Storey

Magic in the Playroom

The toys in the playroom were very friendly with the little folk who lived in the garden. There were fairies and pixies, gnomes and brownies, all merry and happy and friendly.

Sometimes the gnomes came to drink a cup of tea in the dolls' house. Sometimes the pixies came to dance to the music of the little musical box. And sometimes the fairies or the brownies came to play hide-and-seek with the toys.

They did have fun, and the toys always loved to see the pretty heads of the little folk peeping over the window sill. But when a family of goblins came to live in the old oak tree in the garden the toys were not quite so pleased to see them.

"The goblins are not so polite as the fairies," said the pink rabbit, shaking his head.

"The goblins have rather bad manners," said the big doll.

"They make a noise when they eat," said the red-haired doll, who was very particular indeed.

But nobody said anything rude to the goblins and each night they popped in at the window with the other little folk.

Then a horrid thing happened. One night, after the little folk had gone back to the garden, the pink rabbit put his hand up to his collar and found that the little brooch which kept his coat together at the neck was quite gone!

"I believe I saw it peeping out of the pocket of one of the goblins," said the clockwork mouse suddenly.

There was a deep silence. The toys were too shocked for words. To think that one of their guests would steal something!

"You must be wrong, Mouse," said the pink rabbit at last. "My brooch must have dropped somewhere."

So they hunted for it, but it could not be found. "We will not say anything about it at all," said the rabbit. "It is horrid to think that anyone would steal from us."

But after that other things began to go! The red-haired doll missed her necklace! She usually kept it in the kitchen cupboard in the dolls' house – and one night when she went to put it on, it was not in the cup-board! Oh dear!

And worse than that, the walking duck lost her key! It was always kept on a ribbon, tied to her neck, so that it should not be lost. It was easy to wind up the walking duck when she had her key handy like that. But now it was gone! Someone had cut her rib-

bon in half and taken the key, perhaps when she was playing a game and was too excited to notice.

The toys stared at one another in dismay. Something really must be done now! There was no doubt at all that those bad-tempered little goblins had taken their things.

"We will complain to the others," said the duck. "Surely the fairies, the pixies, the brownies and the gnomes will be able to make the goblins give back to us all the things they have stolen!"

So that night the rabbit took Ringding the fairy, Twinks the pixie, Frisk the brownie and Snip the gnome into the kitchen of the dolls' house and shut the door.

"Whatever is the matter?" asked Ringding in alarm, looking at the rabbit's solemn face. "You look as if you have lost a new penny and found a button!"

"I've something to tell you," said the rabbit, "and I don't want the goblins to hear me. Little folk, I am sorry to say that the goblins have been stealing some of our things."

The little folk stared at the pink rabbit in horror. Could it really be true? Ringding went very red indeed. She felt quite cross.

"I don't believe it," she said. "You must have made a mistake, Rabbit."

But when the rabbit told her about his brooch and the red-haired doll's necklace and the walking duck's key, the little folk nodded their heads.

"Yes," said Twinks the pixie. "I believe you, Rabbit. It was only yesterday that I noticed the goblins had a new front door key fitting their lock in the oak tree – and now I come to think of it, it was exactly like the key belonging to the walking duck!"

"What shall we do about it?" asked Frisk the brownie.

"We shall have to use magic on the goblins," said Snip the gnome. "We must make them give up the stolen things somehow."

"But the goblins know more magic than we do," said Ringding. "Whatever spell we do to make them give back what they have stolen will be of no use – for the goblins know much stronger spells than we do!"

"Well, we will try, anyway," said Snip.

So that night, when the goblins had all gone from the playroom into the garden, the little folk went to the oak tree where the goblin family lived and made a spell to force them to give up the stolen goods. But it was no use at all! The goblins put their heads out of their little windows and laughed at them.

"You don't know enough magic!" they shouted. "Stop your silly spells, or we will make a stronger one and turn you into ladybirds!"

The little folk went away. They didn't want to be turned into ladybirds! They told the toys what had happened and everyone was very sad.

The next night the goblins visited the playroom bold as ever – and do you know, although the toys kept a close watch on them to make sure they did not

take anything, those clever goblins managed to steal quite a lot of things.

"Look!" cried the walking duck, peeping into Mummy's work-basket, which she had left in the corner on the floor. "Mummy's little scissors are gone – the ones she cuts button holes with!"

"And all her needles!" cried the rabbit, seeing the needle-case quite empty.

"And her nice steel thimble," cried the clockwork mouse. "Oh, whatever will she say?"

"It is time we did some magic!" said the rabbit suddenly. "I be-lieve I know how to get back the stolen things. Yes, I believe I do!"

He ran to the toy cupboard and pulled out a big magnet that the children sometimes played with. He and the toys slipped out of the window and ran to the oak tree. They banged on the door and, when the goblins opened it, the toys crowded inside.

"Goblins," said the rabbit sternly, "we have come to get back all the things you stole tonight! We have some wonderful magic, much stronger than any you know! Watch!"

The rabbit took the big magnet, which he had been holding behind him, and showed it to the goblins. They laughed at him scornfully.

"That will not find anything!" they said.

The rabbit held out the magnet and then a very strange thing happened. The stolen pair of scissors, which had been hidden under the carpet, suddenly flew up to the magnet and hung on the end of it! Then dozens of needles appeared and flew to the magnet, too! They hung there tightly. And then from a goblin's pocket the thimble flew out and rushed to the magnet as well.

"Aha!" said the rabbit, pleased. "You see what a powerful magic we keep in the playroom, Goblins!"

The goblins turned pale, as they stared in surprise. They had never seen a magnet before, and they were full of fear. They rushed to the door, crowded out and disappeared into the night.

"We shan't see them again," said the rabbit pleased. "Let's just look round and see if we can find anything else they stole."

They hunted around and found all the things they had missed and a few more, too! The walking duck took her key from the front door of the oak tree and tied it on to a new ribbon round her neck. She was very pleased to have it back again.

Then back they all went to the playroom and put the needles, thimble and scissors into the work-basket. They laughed whenever they thought of the goblins' astonishment.

"That magnet was a fine idea," said the pink rabbit, putting it away in the cupboard. "I don't think the goblins will rob toys again. They will be too much afraid of magic in the playroom!"

The Magic Treacle Jug

Now once when Miggle the goblin was walking home at night through Goblin Village, he saw a light in Mother Tick-Tock's cottage window. He stopped and thought for a moment.

"I think I'll go and peep in," he said to himself. "Mother Tick-tock's grandfather was a wizard and it's said that she knows plenty of useful spells. I might see something interesting if I go and peep."

So he crept into the front garden and peeped in at the lighted window. Mother Tick-Tock was there, cutting large slices of bread, one after the other.

"I suppose those are for her children's supper," thought Miggle, counting them. "One, two, three, four, five, six, seven – yes, they are. Goodness me – does she give them just dry bread for their suppers, poor things?"

He watched carefully. He saw Mother Tick-Tock take up a small blue jug and he heard her speak to it.

"Pour me treacle, strong and sweet,
For a Very Special Treat!"

And, to Miggle's surprise, the jug left Mother Tick-Tock's hand, poised itself above a slice of bread and poured out good, thick, yellow treacle! Then it balanced itself above the next slice and poured more treacle. Then it went to the third slice.

"Good gracious me! How can a little jug like that hold so much treacle!" thought Miggle, in surprise. "Look at it, pouring thickly over one slice after another. What lovely treacle too! Ooooh, I wish I had some of it!"

Mother Tick-Tock suddenly caught sight of Miggle's face at the window and, leaving the jug pouring treacle on the last slice of all, she ran to the window, shouting angrily. Miggle disappeared at once and ran home at top speed. He was afraid of Mother Tick-Tock.

But he couldn't forget that wonderful Treacle-Jug. To think of having sweet treacle at any time!

How lucky Mother Tick-Tock's children were. No wonder he so often saw them about with thick slices of bread and treacle.

Now two days later Miggle made himself a fine pudding. But when he came to taste it he found that he had left out the sugar. Ooooh – how horrid it was!

"Now, if only I could borrow that Treacle-Jug!" thought Miggle, longingly. "I could have treacle all over my pudding and it would be one of the nicest I'd ever had. I wonder if Mother Tick-Tock would lend me the jug."

Just at that very moment Miggle saw someone passing his cottage and who should it be but Mother Tick-Tock herself, on her way to visit a friend, Mrs.

Know-A-Lot. Miggle watched her go down the road and a small thought uncurled itself in his mind.

"Couldn't I just borrow the Treacle-Jug for a few minutes? Nobody would know. And if it's a magic jug, the treacle would never, never come to an end, so it wouldn't matter my having just a very little!"

He sat and thought about it, looking at his sugar-less pudding. Then he popped it back into the oven to keep warm and ran out of the front door very quickly indeed. "I must get that jug before I change my mind!"

he thought. "I'll use it to cover my pudding with trea-cle, then I'll take it straight back. Run, Miggle, run!"

He came to Mother Tick-Tock's cottage. The door was locked, but the window was open a crack – a big enough crack for a small goblin to put in a bony arm and reach to the shelf for a small blue jug! There! He had it. But how strange – it was quite empty!

"I'd better not go too fast, in case I fall and break it," he thought. So he put it under his coat and walked back slowly. He felt very excited indeed.

31

He stood the blue jug on his table and fetched his pudding from the oven. "Ha, pudding – you're going to taste very nice in a minute!" he said and set it down in the middle of his table. He picked up the jug and spoke solemnly, as Mother Tick-Tock had.

"Pour me treacle, strong and sweet,
For a Very Special Treat!"

said Miggle. The little jug left his hand at once and poised itself over the pudding. It tilted and – to Miggle's great delight – a stream of rich golden treacle poured out and fell on his pudding. Miggle's mouth began to water. Oooh! That pudding was going to taste very, very nice!

"There! That's enough, thank you, little Treacle-Jug," said Miggle at last. "Don't pour any more, or the treacle will spill out of the dish."

But the jug took no notice at all. It went on pouring steadily and Miggle saw that the treacle was now dripping over the edges of the pudding-dish. "Hey! Didn't you hear what I said!" he cried. "Stop, jug! You'll ruin my tablecloth!"

But the jug didn't stop. It still hung there in the air, treacle pouring from its little spout. Miggle was angry. He snatched at the jug, but it hopped away in the air and went on pouring in another place.

"Stop, jug! Don't pour treacle into my armchair!" shouted Miggle. "Oh my goodness! Look what you've done! Emptied treacle all over the seat of my chair and the cushion! Come away from there!"

He snatched at the jug again, but it wouldn't let itself be caught. It got away from his grabbing hand just in time and hung itself up in the air just above the

wash-tub, which was full of Miggle's dirty clothes, soaking in the suds there.

"Hey!" cried Miggle in alarm. "Not over my washing, for goodness' sake! Stop, I say! Don't you see what you're doing? You're not supposed to pour treacle over chairs and wash-tubs, only over puddings and tarts! Oh, you mischievous jug! Wait till I get you! I'll break you in half!"

He snatched at the jug again, but it swung away in the air and this time hung itself over the nice new hearth-rug.

Trickle, trickle, trickle – the rich, sticky treacle poured down steadily over the rug, and

poor Miggle tried to pull it away. But he soon found himself standing in treacle, for it spread gradually over the floor.

Miggle began to feel very alarmed indeed. What was he to do with this mad Treacle-Jug? He simply MUST stop it somehow.

"Ah – I've an idea!" thought Miggle. "Where's my fishing net? I'll get that and catch the jug in it. Then I'll smash it to bits on the ground. Oh, this treacle! How I hate walking in it! It's just like glue!"

He made his way to the corner where he kept his

net and took hold of it. At once the Treacle-Jug swung itself over to him and poured treacle down on his head and face. How horrible! How sticky! Miggle was so angry that he shouted at the top of his voice.

"I'll smash you! I'll break you into a hundred pieces!" He swung the fishing net at the jug and almost caught it. It seemed frightened and swung away out of the door and up the stairs, pouring treacle all the way. Miggle sat down and cried bitterly. Whatever was he to do?

Soon he heard a curious glug-glug noise and he looked up in alarm. A river of treacle was flowing slowly down the stairs! It flowed through the kitchen and out of the door, down the path and into the street. People passing by were quite astonished.

Mother Tick-Tock, coming back from visiting her friend, was astonished too. But she knew in a trice what had happened.

"Miggle's borrowed my Treacle-Jug!" she said. "I saw him peeping through the window when I used it

the other night. The mean, thieving little fellow!"

Miggle saw Mother Tick-Tock and waded out through the treacly river to his front gate, crying, "Please, Mother Tick-Tock, I'm sorry. I can't make this jug stop pouring. Is there a spell to stop it as well as to start it?"

"Of course there is," said Mother Tick-Tock. "It's just as well to know both spells if you steal something like a Treacle-Jug, Miggle. Well, you can keep the jug if you like. I've a much bigger one I can use. How tired of treacle you must be, Miggle!"

"Oh, Mother Tick-Tock, please, please take your jug away," begged Miggle, kneeling down in the treacle.

"I'll do anything you say, if you only will!"

"Very well. If you come and dig my garden for me all the year round and keep it nice, I'll stop the jug from pouring and take it back," said Mother Tick-Tock. Miggle groaned. He did so hate gardening!

"I'll come," he said. "I don't want to, but I will."

"If you don't, I'll send the jug to pour over your head," said Mother Tick-Tock and everyone laughed. She called loudly, "Treacle-Jug, come here!"

The little blue jug sailed out of a bedroom window and hung over Miggle's head. He dodged away at once. Mother Tick-Tock chanted loudly,

"Be empty, jug, and take yourself
Back to your place upon my shelf!"

And – hey presto – the Treacle-Jug became quite empty, turned itself upside-down to show Mother Tick-Tock that it had obeyed her and then flew swiftly through the air on the way to her cottage. Mother Tick-Tock knew she would find it standing quietly in its place on her kitchen-shelf.

"Well, good-bye, Miggle," she said. "You've a lot of cleaning up to do, haven't you? Somehow I don't think you'll want to eat treacle again in a hurry!"

She was right. Poor old Miggle can't even see a treacle-tin now without running for miles! And I'm not a bit surprised at that!